The Sigh

MARJANE SATRAPI

ARCHAIA ENTERTAINMENT LLC
WWW.ARCHAIA.COM

THE SIGH

Written and Illustrated by
Marjane Satrapi

Translation by **Edward Gauvin**
English Edition design by **Fawn Lau**
Cover Illustration by **Marjane Satrapi**

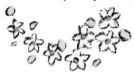

THE SIGH. December 2011. FIRST PRINTING

10 9 8 7 6 5 4 3 2 1

ISBN: 1-936393-46-8
ISBN-13: 978-1-936393-46-6

Published by Archaia
Archaia Entertainment LLC
1680 Vine Street, Suite 1010
Los Angeles, California, 90028, USA
www.archaia.com

Archaia Entertainment, LLC
PJ Bickett, CEO
Mark Smylie, CCO
Mike Kennedy, Publisher
Stephen Christy, Editor-in-Chief

Whether this tale be true or false, none can tell, for none were there to witness it themselves.

Still, they say that once upon a time there lived a merchant who had three daughters. He had raised them on his own as his wife, alas, had passed away.

The eldest was named Orchid, the middle one Violet, and the youngest one Rose. Rose looked just like her dearly departed mother.

Each year, the merchant undertook a long journey for his trade. He traveled the world, paid visits to friends and acquaintances, purchased all manner of items, and above all, brought back many gifts for his children.

That year, like every year, he summoned his daughters as he was preparing to depart. "My beloved children, I leave on the morrow. What would you have me bring back?"

"A dress made of peacock feathers," said Orchid, wriggling unbecomingly.

(I forgot to mention that Orchid, the eldest, was somewhat ugly.)

"A merino shawl!" said Violet, who was always cold.

"The seed of a blue bean," said Rose, who was especially interested in botany.

The next morning, the merchant left on his journey, which took almost two months.

Upon returning, he found his three daughters on the doorstep, delighted to see their father again, and quite excited by the thought of their gifts.

"Welcome back, Papa!"

"Papa darling!"

"Dearest Papa!"

"How happy I am to see you all again! You are my life's true treasures. Come, let us go inside!"

Once they were in the house, the merchant opened his trunks.

"Here is a dress made of peacock feathers for Orchid."

"Oh, Papa! It's incredible! With this dress, the Prince will fall in love with me, and we'll get married!" (Orchid often forgot she was ugly.)

"And a merino shawl for Violet!"

"With this shawl, I'll be sure to be warm in winter. I won't even get the flu this year," said Violet, coughing slightly, for she was a fragile thing.

Then the merchant turned to Rose, paled, blushed, and paled again. "Rose, my child, I have been to all the great markets of the world, where everything can be found. Everything, from hen's milk to the human soul, is for sale there.

"But I could not find you the seed of a blue bean."

"Ah!" sighed Rose, sad not to receive a present.

Suddenly, there was a knock at the door.

Knock, knock, knock!

"Who's there?" asked the merchant, surprised to have a visitor at ten o'clock at night.

"Ah the Sigh!"

"Ah the Sigh? Who's that?"

"Your daughter just summoned me. She said, 'Ah!' I have something for her. Please open the door."

The merchant opened the door.

"Here, sir. This is what caused your daughter to sigh."

He placed the seed of a blue bean in the merchant's hand.

The merchant was so happy that he thanked Ah a hundred times over.

"Mr. Ah, you have no idea how happy you've made my daughter. One day I shall return the favor! My word of honor: if there's anything I can do for you someday, I won't waste a single second!"

"There is nothing I want right now," said Ah the Sigh.

"Just know you can count on me," the merchant repeated.

"Someday, we'll see," Ah replied. And he took his leave.

The happy merchant gave his daughter the seed of the blue bean, which she planted in a pot she'd prepared just for it.

*F*or one year—in other words, 365 days—Rose watered her plant every day. By the time those 365 days had gone by, the plant had grown 365 centimeters, unfurled 365 leaves, and sprouted 365 blue beans.

The day of the blue bean plant's first birthday, at ten o'clock at night, just as the merchant and his three daughters were having a quiet cup of herbal tea, there was a sudden knock at the door.

"Who's there?" the merchant asked, puzzled to be disturbed at so late an hour.

"Ah the Sigh."

"Ah! My friend! What can I do for you?"

"I have come for Rose, to take her away with me."

"Rose? What for?"

"Sadly, I cannot say. But you do remember, I hope, that one year ago to this very day, you promised to grant my wish."

"Yes of course, but I never said I'd give you my daughter," said the merchant, at once surprised and worried.

"You said you would grant my any wish, no matter what!" the Sigh replied.

From a hiding place upstairs the merchant pulled out a great sack of gold coins and precious gems, which he brought to Ah the Sigh, who was waiting at the door.

"Here! I'll give you all the money you want, but don't ask me for my daughter!"

"Sir," said Ah, "I know you are a great trader, but let me say this: money isn't the answer to everything in life, and besides, I didn't come all this way to beg. I must take your daughter away with me."

"Over my dead body," the merchant declared.

"Don't be stupid. I'm no killer, and you want to live. Honor your promises," Ah replied.

A good negotiator, the merchant tried everything, but Ah the Sigh stood firm.

Finally, as no amicable agreement could be reached, the two came to blows.

On seeing this, Rose decided to intervene.

"Please, Papa, it's all right. I'll go with Mr. Ah."

"But sweetheart, you don't know what fate this vile creature has in store for you," the merchant said.

At that, Ah the Sigh gave a start.

"Oh, my, my! You, sir! You've been around the world ten times and seen it all. Do I really look evil or wicked to you?" Then he added, "I assure you, no harm shall befall your daughter."

At last, after lengthy discussion, the merchant agreed to deliver his daughter into the Sigh's hands. It must be said he had little choice in the matter. He had given his word, and a man's word is his bond.

Ah the Sigh put a blindfold over Rose's eyes.

Together they climbed onto the back of a horse and, for three days, traveled over mountain, sea, and plain.

"Here we are, Miss Rose," said the Sigh. "You can take off your blindfold."

And so Rose discovered her new home: a great palace, magnificent gardens, trees, bushes, streams, plants, servants, fountains…

It's wonderful, thought Rose, who had a hard time hiding her wonder before such beauty.

The days went by, and Rose spent them in a variety of ways: a morning milk bath and then a massage, a facial after that, and then a manicure, riding, swimming, reading, botanical research, a live performance every evening—in short, everything she could ever dream of having.

Everything but one thing: she missed her family terribly.

And so it came about that after one month, she made her distress known.

"Ah!"

"Here I am, Mistress. Your wish is my command. What do you require?"

"I miss my father and my sisters. I'd like to pay them a visit."

Ah the Sigh put the blindfold over her eyes. They climbed on a horse and, for three days, traveled over mountain, sea, and plain.

Knock knock knock!

"Who's there?" came the merchant's gloomy voice.

"Father, it's me, Rose!"

What a reunion! The merchant wept tears of happiness. Orchid and Violet let out little hysterical cries. In short, the whole house was filled with joy once more.

Rose, too, was delighted to be back with her family.

That evening after dinner, her sisters surrounded her and peppered her with questions.

"So how is it?" Orchid asked.

"Wonderful, to tell the truth! I'm taken care of. I do my studies, devote myself to my plants, get exercise, and have servants—"

"But?" Violet insisted.

"But nothing!" Rose replied.

"There must be some sort of trick," Violet retorted.

"Tell me, Rose," said Orchid with an exceptionally intelligent air, "are you given something to drink every evening?"

"Uh... yes, every night I drink a cup of herbal tea with honey and jasmine, and let me tell you, I sleep like a baby!

"I'll bring you some next time!" promised Rose.

"Listen, little sister: next time you're back home, don't drink the tea. Just pour it out under the rug. Cut your pointer finger with a knife and put salt on the wound. It'll hurt—you'll see—and keep you from sleeping. Then wait and see what happens," said Orchid.

The father and the three sisters spent a marvelous evening together, and once morning came, Rose returned to her palace.

As soon as she was back, Rose followed her oldest sister's advice to the letter: she poured the tea out under the rug, cut her pointer finger, put salt on the wound—my God, that hurt!—then got into bed and waited...

Orchid was right: at the stroke of midnight, the door to her room opened softly.

R ose pretended to be asleep. She lifted her left eyelid slightly and saw a very handsome young man coming toward her bed. He sat down, and began gently to caress her hair.

Rose leapt up.

"Who are you, and what are you doing in my room?"

"What do you mean, who am I? And why aren't you sleeping, anyway?" said the young man.

"I know what you were up to with the tea! So I didn't drink it. Besides, I asked first! Now answer me, who are you? Make it fast, or I'll call the servants."

The young man lowered his head and said:

"I will explain everything. I am the Prince of the Kingdom of Sighs. When you called on my aid a little over a year ago for your seed of a blue bean, I fell in love with you at once. I spent a year trying to forget you, but I could not. So I sent my man to fetch you. But I know humans well. They are all unfaithful. I was so afraid to lose you that I preferred never to show myself. I made do with admiring you from afar. Since your arrival in my land, I have come each night to caress your beautiful red hair…

"Now you know everything! If you wish to leave, I will not stop you."

Faced with the Prince's kindness and handsomeness, what could Rose do? Nothing! So that is exactly what she did, and gave him a kiss.

Now they were officially in love.

*T*he next day, Rose and the Prince took their breakfast together and discussed their plans for the future. Then Rose said:

"My prince, I'd like us to take a walk in our wonderful garden. I think I'd find it even more wonderful still by your side. And there's something I want to show you—something I planted when I got here."

"Of course, Rose," said the Prince, and offered her his arm. "Your love for nature is something that only brings us closer together."

They walked all over. The Prince showed Rose hidden paths and corners. Suddenly, Rose noticed a cascade of mauve flowers she'd never seen before.

"Look at those! I've never seen anything so beautiful before in my life!"

The Prince bent over to pick a bouquet for his beloved. Rose, who was watching attentively, suddenly noticed a tiny feather in the Prince's armpit. Delicately, she plucked the feather and the unthinkable happened.

The sky grew black. There was lightning and tornadoes, then a downpour of hot, almost burning rain; flowers wilted, trees shed their leaves, and the Prince fell lifeless to the ground.

"AHHHH!" Rose cried.

"What have you done, Mistress?" said Ah the Sigh, who had appeared at her cry.

"I don't know! I saw a tiny feather in his armpit– " Sobs kept her from finishing her sentence.

"Don't tell me you plucked the feather!"

"Yesssss!"

"But Mistress, that was the breath of life! You have taken it from him! You have killed the prince!"

"What must I do, Ah? What must I do?"

"It is I who should be asking you that question. We must find the feather that the storm carried away. Unfortunately, with all these petals and leaves strewn over a hundred acres of garden, that's near impossible!"

Rose started sobbing even harder.

"What a fool I am!" she cried.

"You can say that again. But the damage is done. What shall we do now?"

To punish herself, Rose replied, "Take me to the slave market and sell me!"

And so it was done.

*A*t the first house she was sold to, Rose became a cook in the kitchens. The other servants told her that two years ago, the son of the lady of the house, her only child, had disappeared. Apparently, there was no word of him.

Since then, the lady of the house had worn only black, as a sign of mourning.

Poor woman! Rose thought.

To cheer her up, Rose prepared delicious dishes whose recipes her father had brought back from distant lands... but it was all for naught.

The lady of the house had no appetite. Nothing seemed to please her.

Once dinner was over, Rose cleared the dishes, washed them, cleaned the kitchen, and retired at last to the maids' quarters, where the other nine servants were already sleeping. Then she began to dream of her Prince. A single tear ran down the length of her face, which was marked by sadness.

That night, something strange happened around two o'clock in the morning; the head housekeeper left the room and did not return till dawn.

The second night, after finishing her duties, Rose climbed in bed. Once more, the housekeeper left the room, and once more, she did not return until first light.

The third night, Rose decided to follow her. The housekeeper stopped beside the fountain and turned to face it. Rose, hiding behind a tree, heard her say three words aloud :

"Adji, Madji, la Tarradji!"

Probably magic words! thought Rose.

And she was right!

The fountain split in two and opened up. A stairway appeared, and Rose saw the housekeeper go down, lantern in hand. The fountain immediately shut behind her. It goes without saying that Rose imitated her right away: she too stood facing the fountain and said the three magic words out loud. The fountain opened once more, and Rose went down the steps.

She walked down a long, damp corridor at the end of which she saw the housekeeper with a young man, handsome as the moon, chained to the wall.

Rose hid in the shadows. The housekeeper held a whip in her hand.

She said, "Well, have you made up your mind? Are you going to marry me yet?"

"Never in my life!" cried the young man. "I'd rather die!"

The housekeeper grew angry, and whipped him as hard as she could. When at last she grew tired, she stopped.

Then she said, "I'll be back tomorrow night! Think carefully. Either marry me, or spend the rest of your days in this hole!"

The young man said nothing.

Rose hurried off, taking the steps four at a time, and got out just before the housekeeper. Her heart was beating madly. Now she understood everything: that woman had kidnapped the son of the lady of the house, and wanted to force him to marry her.

What a monster that housekeeper is, thought Rose.

The next morning, Rose went to her mistress and told her:

"Mistress, I had a very strange dream last night. I dreamed that someone said three magic words before the fountain, and it opened. There were steps, then a hallway, and at the end of the hallway, a room with your son in it."

"Don't talk nonsense, Rose," her mistress replied.

"But Mistress, doesn't your son have three moles in the middle of his chest?"

This question gave the lady of the house a start.

"How do you know that?"

"I told you. I dreamt it!"

"If your dream is right, perhaps I'll find my son under that accursed fountain!"

Rose and her mistress were now in the garden, followed by the housekeeper.

Rose stood before the fountain and recited the magic words: "Adji, Madji, la Tarradji!"

The housekeeper's complexion changed. She was green with fear.

The two women descended the stairs and went down the hallway. At last, the lady of the house found her son, pale and emaciated after two years of torture and starvation. The young man told his mother everything. Furious, the lady of the house went back up to the garden and ordered the house-keeper tied to a horse's tail by her hair. The horse was sent galloping off toward unknown deserts.

Once rid of her horrible servant, the lady of the house turned to Rose and said:

"Dear child, you have returned my son to me and saved his life. Would you like to marry him and become my daughter-in-law?"

"Mistress, I love another man. I could never marry your son," Rose replied.

"Then make a wish and I shall fulfill it."

So Rose said:

"Give me back my freedom. I did not find a cure for what ails me here, and so I must go."

And her mistress gave her back her freedom.

Rose called the Sigh.

"Ah!"

"Yes Mistress, here I am. Your wish is my command. What do you require?"

"Sell me once more in another slave market."

And so Rose went on her way again.

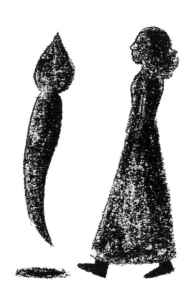

his time, she wound up at an old astrologer's. He had lost his wife, and had but one son. Rose became his gardener. In a few days, she had already come to know everyone who lived in the house except the astrologer's son, whom she still hadn't met. On the eighth day, she finally asked the cook:

"They say the astrologer has a son, but I've never seen him."

"Oh dearie, if you only knew! The astrologer's son is a dragon. Every day, I have to roast a whole sheep and two chickens to satisfy him." The cook added, "He's far too dangerous. So dangerous that no one, not even the master, dares enter his chamber. We drop his food down the chimney to get it to him."

Rose gave the matter some thought. It seemed impossible to her that the astrologer and his wife—that is to say, two humans—could have brought a dragon into the world. She decided to solve the mystery and marched straight to the observatory where the astrologer spent almost all his time.

She told him: "Master, have a leather bag made and put me inside. Tomorrow at lunch, drop me down the chimney to the dragon, your son."

"Who told you that story?" asked the astrologer.

"That's not important," Rose replied. "Tomorrow I will go see your son."

"Poor girl—you've lost your wits! My son is quite dangerous. What you're suggesting is suicide!"

But at Rose's insistence, the astrologer relented.

The next day at noon, the servants lowered Rose in a leather bag down the chimney into the dragon's chamber.

When the bag hit the floor, the dragon roared:

"A human being in my room!? Get out of your bag so I can eat you!"

"Why don't you get out of your bag?"

"What bag? I'm a dragon!"

"Fine, so you don't have a bag, but you have a shell. Get out of your shell!"

The dragon resisted, but Rose would not let up. Finally, after two hours of back-and-forth, the dragon said:

"I'll count to three, and we'll both come out!"

Rose, who took every precaution, said:

"How do I know you'll keep your word?"

The dragon grew wrathful and said:

"Miss, I will not permit you to doubt my word. I'm counting! One, two, three—"

Rose decided to trust him, and out they both came from their hiding places. The astrologer's son was, in reality, a handsome young man who'd hidden himself in the skin of a dragon.

The astrologer, who'd seen the whole thing through the window, leapt into the room and took his son into his arms.

His son said, "Father, after Mother died, I felt so alone, and you were always so busy watching the stars that you didn't see my sadness. If I crawled into the skin of a dragon, it was to protect myself."

"From now on, you'll have my full attention!" his father replied. "It's all my fault, son—forgive me!"

Then the astrologer turned toward Rose and asked for her hand in marriage for his son.

"I love another, Master. If you wish to thank me, give me back my freedom. I must find another remedy for my misfortune, and alas, it lies not in your house."

Rose was freed.

"Ah," Rose sighed, "take me to the slave market and sell me!"

his time, Rose became the maid to a couple. In their house, custom had it that each new servant would spend three nights at the foot of the couple's bed. The first night, Rose was filled as usual with thoughts of her prince, and did not manage to fall asleep.

Suddenly, at the stroke of midnight, she saw something horrifying: the wife took a sword and cut her husband's head clean off. Then she got dressed up to the nines and left.

Rose was so frozen with fear that she almost stopped breathing.

Just before sunrise, the wife reappeared, put the poor man's head back in place, and from a box, took out a tiny feather, which she dipped in a bowl of oil. Then she passed the feather lightly around her husband's neck.

Her husband sneezed, then woke up and asked his wife:

"Where have you been? Your body's all cold!"

His wife, who had a lot of nerve, answered:

"What a question! That dinner was no good, and I was in the bathroom all night! You were sleeping like a rock. You had no idea how sick I was!"

"I'm sorry, dear, I'm sorry..."

He went back to sleep, and soon, so did his wife.

The next night, the same thing happened.

The third night, Rose couldn't stifle her curiosity any longer.

She resolved to overcome her fear and follow the wife to see what she was up to.

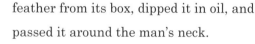

Once she was outside—after having cut her husband's head off, like every other night—the wife got on a horse. Rose took another from the stable and followed her at a distance, so as not to be seen or heard. They rode through a forest, and finally stopped before a great cabin. The wife got off her horse and joined almost a dozen men who, from the looks of it, had been waiting for her inside. Rose pressed her ear to the side of the house and listened.

First she heard what sounded like quite a party, which went on for more than an hour. Then the wife told the men that her husband would soon leave her his entire fortune.

Rose understood at once: the ten men were bandits, and the wife their chief. She'd married the man to strip him of all his belongings. Rose could not let such an injustice stand.

She got back in her saddle and galloped as fast as she could. Once back at the house, she put the man's head back in place, took the feather from its box, dipped it in oil, and passed it around the man's neck.

"Aachoo!" the man sneezed. "Rose, what are you doing here? Where's my wife?"

"Master, wake up! Quickly, we haven't much time!"

Convinced his wife was in danger, the man dressed in under a minute.

"Take your sword," said Rose.

A short while later, the man and Rose stood before the bandits' cabin. Through the window, the master saw his wife singing.

"He's dumber than a box of rocks,
His breath smells like old sweaty socks,
But all I want from him is his money."

The ten bandits sang the refrain "*his money, his money*" in chorus.

The man was so enraged he saw red. He burst into the cabin, drew his sword, and killed the ten men one after another.

Then he said to his wife: "I have loved you so much I can't kill you. Go, now. Disappear! Don't ever let me see you again!"

His wife didn't even try to make excuses. She left.

The man thanked Rose for having shown him the truth. Disgusted with marriage, he did not ask for her hand.

"You have saved my honor and my life. Tell me what would make you happy, and I will give it to you: gold, money, diamonds…"

"None of that," Rose replied. "Just give me the feather and the pot of oil."

As soon as they were back at the house, the man gave her what she'd asked for without batting an eye.

"Ah!" said Rose.

"Mistress, there are no more slave markets. Slavery has just been abolished," said Ah the Sigh.

"Who said anything about slave markets? Take me back to our Kingdom, Ah."

ose traveled over mountains, across seas, through plains, and finally returned to her Kingdom. It was just as she had left it a month earlier. The Prince's body lay unmoving in the middle of a magnificent mausoleum. She drew near it, took the feather, dipped it in oil, and placed it under his arm.

"Aachoo!" the Prince sneezed.

At the sound of his sneeze, all the flowers grew beautiful once more.

The trees donned their leaves again, and the sun took its place up in the sky.

"Rose, are you there?"

"Yes, my Prince. I am here, and here I will be forevermore."

"By taking away my feather, you took the breath of life from me. I don't know how you ever found it again!"

"I'll tell you some other time. The important part is that you're near me now," said Rose.

"Life hangs from so slender a thread. Life is but a sigh…"

MARJANE SATRAPI

was born in Iran in 1969. She was raised during a tumultuous time in Iranian history, witnessing the Iranian Revolution and its many politcal and socially suppressive consequences. This left a lasting impression on her, and she chronicled her experiences in her multi-award winning autobiographical graphic novels, *Persepolis* and *Persepolis 2*. Now residing in France, Marjane continues to produce thought-provoking works that raise awareness to the human condition.